Be a Cave Explorer!

Contents

Written by Catherine Baker

Collins

Fantastic caves

Lots of people visit caves each year – for good reasons.

Caves are astonishing! They are fun for families ... and sports people.

How caves were made

Some caves were formed by the sea.

Strong waves crashed on this beach, turning the rocks into caves.

Some caves were made when
rain leaked into rock.

6

The rain made the rock weak, so caves formed.

Exploring caves

By exploring caves, experts can tell us their stories.

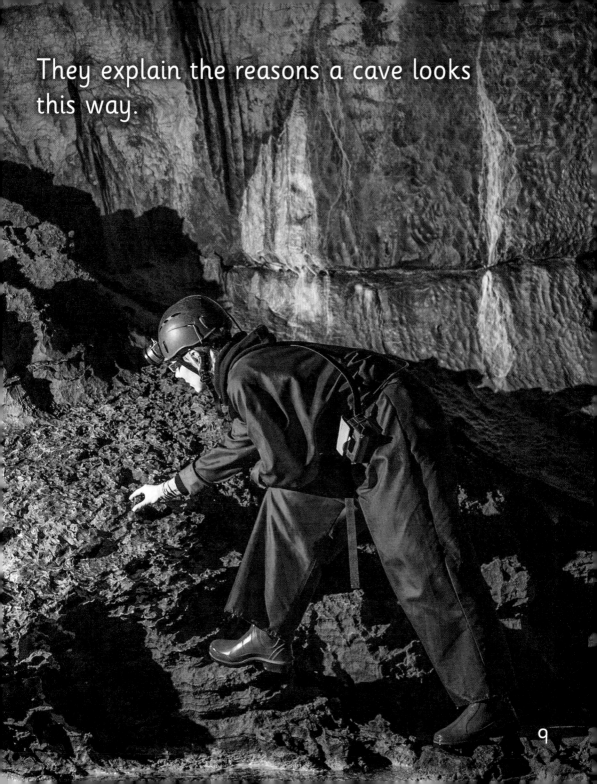

They explain the reasons a cave looks this way.

There are lots of ways of exploring caves.

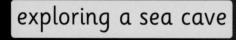
exploring a sea cave

clambering up rock

a team travelling down a stream

11

Biggest and best

This is the biggest cave
people can visit.

Its name is Hang Son Doong.
There is a real forest in it!

The steps lead to the longest chain of caves you can visit.

Explorers have still not reached the end of it!

Mammoth Cave

This cave looks like a dream, but it is real!

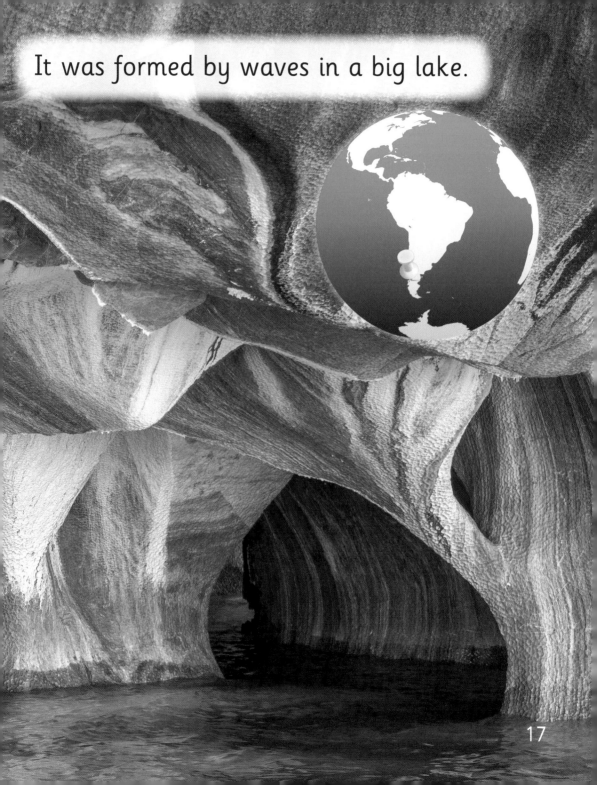

It was formed by waves in a big lake.

Caves made by people

Do you dream of living in a cave?

People have been living here for at least 3000 years.

Cave kit

There are lots of caves that families can visit!

This is what you may need.

torch

helmet

coat

boots

21

After reading

Letters and Sounds: Phase 5

Word count: 214

Focus phonemes: /ai/ ay, ey, a-e /ee/ ie, ea

Common exception words: the, by, of, are, were, into, when, so, their, have, do, people, you, there, some, here, be, what, to, was

Curriculum links: Human and physical geography

National Curriculum learning objectives: Reading/word reading: read other words of more than one syllable that contain taught GPCs; Reading/comprehension: understand both the books they can already read accurately and fluently and those they listen to by checking that the text makes sense to them as they read, and correcting inaccurate reading

Developing fluency

- Your child may enjoy hearing you read the book.
- Take turns reading a page. Check that your child pauses at commas.

Phonic practice

- Focus on spellings of /ai/ and /ee/ sounds.
- Look together at pages 4–5. Ask your child to find words with the /ai/ sound. (**cave**, **made**, **waves**) Turn to page 6. Can your child find the /ai/ sound but spelt differently? (ai – **rain**)
- Look together at page 2. Ask your child to find the three words that contain the /ee/ sound. Ask them to point to the letters that make this sound in each word. (eo spelling, common exception word: **people**; ea spelling: **each**, **reasons**)

Extending vocabulary

- Look together at page 16 and ask your child to explain the meanings of **dream** and **real**. Ask: Can you think of a synonym for "like a dream"? (e.g. *fantastical, imaginary*)

Comprehension

- Turn to pages 22 and 23 and use the pictures to talk about the different caves explored in this book. Which is your child's favourite cave?
- Ask your child:
  o On pages 4–5 and 6 in what ways are caves formed? (*sea against the cliffs, leaking rain*)
  o On page 8, what sort of stories might a cave tell? (e.g. *how it was formed and why it looks the way it does*)